For Alex, who canoed with me down the Missouri River
—B.C.S.

To Mom and Dad for teaching me to love the sea,
and to Maggie and David for helping us travel across it
—C.S.

Text copyright © 2019 by Brianna Caplan Sayres
Jacket art and interior illustrations copyright © 2019 by Christian Slade

Visit us on the Web! rhcbooks.com

Educators and librarians, for a variety of teaching tools, visit us at RHTeachersLibrarians.com

Library of Congress Cataloging-in-Publication Data
Names: Sayres, Brianna Caplan, author. | Slade, Christian, illustrator.
Title: Where do speedboats sleep at night? / by Brianna Caplan Sayres ;
illustrated by Christian Slade.
Description: First edition. | New York : Random House, [2019]
Summary: Illustrations and rhyming text reveal what sailboats, cruise ships, canoes,
and other vessels do to get ready for bed after a hard day's work.
Identifiers: LCCN 2018005207 (print) | LCCN 2018013387 (ebook) |
ISBN 978-1-5247-6575-0 (hardcover) | ISBN 978-1-5247-6576-7 (hardcover library binding) |
ISBN 978-1-5247-6577-4 (ebook)
Subjects: | CYAC: Stories in rhyme. | Boats and boating—Fiction. | Bedtime—Fiction.
Classification: LCC PZ8.3.S274 (ebook) | LCC PZ8.3.S274 Whm 2019 (print) |
DDC [E]—dc23

MANUFACTURED IN CHINA
10 9 8 7 6 5 4 3 2 1
First Edition

Where Do Speedboats Sleep at Night?

by Brianna Caplan Sayres · illustrated by Christian Slade

Random House 🏠 New York

Where do speedboats sleep at night
after a day of nonstop speeding?
Do moms say, "Turn off your motor—
it's time for bedtime reading"?

Where do sailboats sleep at night
after tacking here, then there?
Do dads say, "Ahoy! Look starboard!
There's Captain Teddy Bear"?

Where do fireboats sleep at night
once fire hoses stop their gushing?
Do they use Mom's spraying water
for their bathing and teeth brushing?

Where do cruise ships sleep at night
once their ports have all been reached?
Do these boats begin to dream
of their own trips to the beach?

Where do canoes sleep at night
after gliding 'cross the lake?
Do dads say, "Put down your paddles!
How come you're still awake?"

Where do tugboats sleep at night
after a day of push and pull?
Do moms say, "Tow in your toys, kids—
Toy Harbor's almost full"?

Where do coast guard boats sleep
after rescues are completed?
Do dads say, "Use my searchlight
as a night-light if you need it"?

Where do ferryboats sleep
once they deliver folks and cars?
Do they stop their back-and-forth trips
and float beneath the stars?

Where do carriers sleep at night
once they've crossed the ocean deep?
Do they cover jets with blankies
and rock them all to sleep?

Where do submarines sleep
when they dive beneath the waves?
Do they fall asleep to stunning views
of underwater caves?

Where do all these boats sleep
once their trips are at their end?
Do they dock in a marina
or perhaps a river bend?

Are they anchored on an inlet
as they take a break from cruising?
Do all these young ships dream of trips
as parents watch them snoozing?

Where do your boats sleep at night
when the time for bed is here?
You'll sleep cozy in your cabin
while they're docked by Bathtub Pier!